To my mom, the best in the world, Judith Alice Mammano.

In loving memory of my dad, Louis George Mammano, 1927–2004.

Special thanks to Station 49 of the Los Angeles County Fire Department

in the research of this book.

Book design by Mary Beth Fiorentino.

Typeset in Gill Sans and ITC Officina.

The illustrations in this book were rendered in watercolor.

Manufactured in Hong Kong.

Library of Congress Cataloging-in-Publication Data

Mammano, Julie.

Rhinos who rescue / by Julie Mammano.

p. cm.

Summary: Rhinoceroses fight fires, save people from drowning,
and assist on the scene of a multi-car accident. Includes a glossary
of firefighting lingo.

ISBN-13: 978-0-8118-5419-1

ISBN-10: 0-8118-5419-1

[1. Fire fighters—Fiction. 2. Rhinoceroses—Fiction.] I. Title.

PZ7.M3117Rc 2007

[E]—dc22

2006009838

Distributed in Canada by Raincoast Books

9050 Shaughnessy Street, Vancouver, British Columbia V6P 6E5

10 9 8 7 6 5 4 3 2 1

Chronicle Books LLC

680 Second Street, San Francisco, California 94107

www.chroniclekids.com

Rhinos Who Rescue

JULIE MAMMANO

A huge HEADER is LOOMING.

In FULL TURNOUTS rhinos get to w**.t.e,a...-M.....

They **MAKE THE HYDRANT** and **PAY OUT** the hoses.

It's time to put up the STICK.

Rhinos who rescue go on **CALLS** rain or shine. They get the **9-1-1** for **SWIFT-WATER RESCUES.**

They are SMOKE JUMPERS

in a CAMP CREW.

In a **WILDFIRE, THE HEAT IS ON.**

They are HEROES.

But there's always room for CRAMMING.

Rescue Rap

Bell alarm

Same-day service hurry up

Rig fire truck or fire engine

Bolt go fast

Blaze fire

Ramp it wait at the ramp (driveway) in case the call is canceled

Header a big cloud of smoke that fills the sky

Looming up ahead

Full turnouts the protective clothing firefighters wear to fight fires

Pumped excited, ready to go

Make the hydrant get the hydrant ready to use

Pay out unload

Stick a long ladder atop a fire truck

Sizing up looking

Major rager huge fire

Throw the ladder put the ladder up to the building

Well-involved swallowed up in flames

Gomers people who play with matches

Calls rescue jobs

9-1-1 emergency call

Swift-water rescue rescue done in rushing water

Smoke jumpers firefighters who parachute into a forest fire

Camp crew firefighters who live in tents in the forest while fighting a forest fire

Wildfire an out-of-control forest fire

The heat is on there's pressure to get the job done quickly

Gnarly bad, dangerous

Pileups bad wrecks with lots of cars

Heroes brave people who save others from danger

All hands working a really big job, all firefighters are needed

Band-aid calls jobs that aren't dangerous

Firehouse the place where firefighters live and fire-fighting equipment is kept

Slug around be lazy

Cramming joking around

AP floor garage where the rigs are parked